For Vinny, Zac, Ella, Jake,
Bea, Louis and Anna
CH

For Linda, Euan, Blair, Conon,
Albhie, Sorley and Marsaili
EM

CHRIS HIGGINS

W/D SALE

TROUBLE AT SCHOOL

Illustrated by
Emily MacKenzie

FIRST DAY

Bella was too excited to eat her breakfast.

Today was the day she was starting her new school. She'd been looking forward to it for weeks.

Moving to an old cottage in the countryside had felt strange at first. Especially as it was the middle of the summer holidays.

But then Bella and her little brother Sid had met Magda and they'd soon settled in. Magda was fun and it was nice having a best friend who lived next door.

Now the holidays were over and it was time to start school. Bella loved school. She couldn't wait to meet her teacher and make new friends.

Magda would always be her very best friend though. Even if she did get Bella into trouble sometimes.

Quite a lot of times actually.

Like the time she climbed up the chimney and covered Bella's living room in soot.

Or the time Bella had fallen through the floor of the attic to her parents' bedroom below and brought the ceiling tumbling down with her. That had been Magda's fault too. She was the one who'd made Bella go up to the attic to look for ghosts. But it was Bella who'd got into trouble.

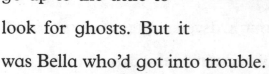

Bella's mum said Magda was a trouble magnet but Bella was glad she had Magda to stick close to. They were going to sit together in class.

"Eat up your breakfast, Bella. You don't want to be late on your first day.

First impressions count," said Mum. "Sid? Where's your bag?"

Bella gulped down her cereal, taking care not to drip milk on her spotless school uniform, while Sid wandered off in search of his backpack.

She knew exactly where *her* bag was: ready and waiting by the front door, where she'd placed it last night.

Inside it was her brand new rough book and her brand new pencil case – and inside that were brand new pens, pencils, felt tips, a rubber and a sharpener.

Next to it was her PE kit, her swimming kit, her book bag and her lunch box.

Bella liked to be prepared. Then she knew that nothing could go wrong.

She took a look in the mirror and was pleased with what she saw. Mum had tied her unruly hair back neatly into pretty cornrows and the navy blue and yellow ribbons matched her navy blue and yellow uniform.

Time to go. Bella picked up her bags, which was easier said than done. There were so many she kept dropping them.

Mum scooped them up with the rest of Sid's bags and chucked them all in the boot of the car. "We never had this much stuff when I was at school! Get in, Bella. Sid? Where have you got to?"

Bella's chest tightened. She didn't want to be late on her first day.

Sid came running out of the house with his backpack and jumped in the back of the car.

Bella breathed a sigh of relief. She was glad Mum was taking them to school on their first day because then she knew that they'd get there on time.

Like Mum said, it was important to make a good first impression.

Mum started the car. Then Bella remembered.

"Stop!" she shouted. "What about Magda?"

DON'T BE LATE

"What *about* Magda?" repeated Mum.

"She asked for a lift!" said Bella.

"Did she?" Mum looked surprised. "She never asked me!"

Come to think of it, she hadn't *asked* anyone, thought Bella. Magda had *told* her it was a good idea that her mum was taking them to school on the first day of term because it meant *she* could have a lift as well.

"Go and get her then," sighed Mum, and she switched off the engine.

Bella jumped out and pressed the bell on Magda's front door.

It didn't work. So she lifted the old iron knocker instead and banged it hard.

No answer.

She banged it again.

And again.

Bella lifted the letter box and peered inside. "Magda!" she shouted. "Come on! We'll be late for school!"

Above her, a bedroom window flew open and a head appeared. It belonged to Babcia.

"Is school today?" she enquired.

Babcia was Magda's grandmother. Round and wrinkled like an old apple, her hair was still in its night-time curlers.

"Yes," said Bella.

"One minute," said Babcia politely, then she roared, "*MAGDA!* GET UP! IS SCHOOL!"

Bella and Sid sat in the car and waited and waited, while Bella's mum repeated words under her breath that *they* would get into BIG TROUBLE for saying.

At last the door opened and Magda
zoomed out, hair flying, shoes undone,
clutching a paper bag.

"Thanks, Mrs Button!" she said, squeezing in between Bella and Sid. "Mum and Dad left for work early this morning and Babcia and I slept in! She said I could eat my breakfast on the way so I wouldn't keep you waiting, if that's OK with you."

Without waiting for an answer, Magda opened the paper bag and peered inside. "Mmm! Yoghurt and toast."

She dumped the toast in Bella's lap, saying, "Hold that while I eat my yoghurt," and yanked the top off the yoghurt pot.

"Oops! Sorry!" she said, as it shot all over Bella.

Magda tried to clean it up, spooning and swallowing yoghurt as fast as she could, but she only made it worse. Bella's new yellow polo shirt and navy cardigan were splattered with cherry-red yoghurt.

Mum passed Bella a handful of tissues and, between them, Bella and Magda dabbed it dry.

Dry but sticky.

"Phew! That's better," said Magda. "Can I have my toast now?"

Magda's toast was stuck upside down to Bella's skirt. Bella pulled it off and handed it to her friend without a word. Yellow butter, orange marmalade and brown toast crumbs clung to her navy school skirt in a smeary mess.

Bella tried hard not to cry.

GETTING LOST

By the time they got to school and Mum had cleaned Bella up as best she could, everybody had gone in.

"Hurry up!" said Magda, hopping about impatiently. "Mr Smart will tell us off if we're late."

The three children dashed through the front door. Well, Magda dashed and Bella and Sid waddled, weighed down by their bags.

cutting it fine," said the lady on reception. "The bell's about to go. Straight to your classrooms please."

Thank goodness I'm with Magda, thought Bella, *or I wouldn't know where to go*.

"Bella," said Sid, "I don't know where to go."

Bella's heart sank. What should she do now? Luckily, Magda had the answer.

"He'll be in Year One. That's Mrs Goodenough's class, down there on the right. Her name's on the door. You'd better take him in, Bella."

"Aren't you coming with us?" asked Bella.

"No," said Magda. "I'll go and tell Mr Smart what you're doing and then you won't get into trouble."

That sounded sensible.

"Be quick!" warned Magda. "I've heard he goes bananas if you're late." And she dashed off to class before the bell went.

Bella and Sid waddled down the corridor with their bags.

They could hear the noise coming from Mrs Goodenough's classroom long before they got there. A clash of children's voices,

rising and falling, talking and *[torn]* laughing and crying. And over it all, *[torn]* much, much BIGGER voice, louder than all the others put together, directing, comforting, instructing.

Bella took a deep breath and pushed open the door.

erywhere. Sitting on ables, ...g on the floor, climbing on the cupboards, drawing on the board.

In the middle of it all a lady was kneeling, helping a small boy to tie his shoelaces. She was a big lady with a kind face, and a mass of black, curly hair not unlike Bella's. She was wearing long, dangly earrings and a brightly coloured dress that flowed out around her.

"Hello," she boomed, looking up with a smile. "Who are you?"

"I'm Sid and this is Bella," announced Sid, looking around with interest. "I can tie my own shoelaces."

"Well, you're a welcome addition to this classroom then. Maybe you'd like to show

William how to do it," said
Mrs Goodenough.

Sid sat down
happily on the
floor to help him.

"Drop your
bags in the
corner by the

pegs, Bella dear, and we'll see to them
afterwards," said Mrs Goodenough.
"Then find yourself somewhere to sit."

Bella opened her mouth to let Mrs
Goodenough know that, actually, she
wasn't in her class, but the teacher had
swung past her to rescue an adventurous
child from the top of the filing cabinet.

So Bella did what she nearly always

did, which is what she was told. She placed her bags in the corner and sat down on a chair to wait till she could get the teacher's attention.

Only it wasn't that easy. Mrs Goodenough was like a tornado, whirling and wheeling around her crazy classroom, wiping noses, breaking up fights, cuddling away tears, refereeing arguments and cleaning up all sorts of interesting spillages.

Bella was far too polite to interrupt and not nearly brave enough to leave without permission.

And because Bella was so quiet and good, and the much younger children in Year One were so loud and noisy, the teacher forgot all about her.

So there she remained, watching the minutes tick by, slowly and surely, till playtime.

SPIN AROUND

Magda marched across to Bella, who was surrounded by Sid and the rest of Year One in the playground. "Where've you been?" she demanded.

"I got stuck in Mrs Goodenough's class," explained Bella.

"I wish I was stuck in Mrs Goodenough's class," said Magda with feeling.

"Did you explain to Mr Smart where I was?" asked Bella.

"No," said Magda. "He wouldn't let me.

You're not allowed to speak in Mr Smart's classroom. Unless you're Mr Smart."

"Why not?"

"Because he's strict. He's got rules – loads of them. We've got to learn them off by heart. I know the first three already: be punctual, wear your uniform with pride, be prepared."

"Oh flip!" said Bella nervously. "What should we do?"

"Let's play Spin Around," said Magda.

And even though that's not what Bella had meant, she found herself asking, "What's Spin Around?"

"I'll show you. Hold my hand. Now, you take her hand."

Magda pointed to Sophie, the little girl

who'd had to be rescued from the top of
the filing cabinet. Bella did as she was
told.

"Now someone grab her other hand,"
instructed Magda.

Sid took it, then William took Sid's and
then everybody else wanted to join in too.
And so it went on, until everyone from
Year One was standing there in a long
line, holding hands.

Bella couldn't help thinking that Magda would make a very good teacher. Better than Mrs Goodenough, actually. There was something about Magda that made you obey her orders.

"Is that it?" she asked.

"No," said Magda. "Hold tight and don't let go."

She started running round in a circle and everyone else had to follow because they were holding hands. The further down the chain you were, the bigger the circle was.

It was fun.

At first.

Soon they were going faster and faster, and the smaller children started shrieking with excitement as their feet barely touched the ground. The ones on the end looked as though they were flying!

But, as they spun out of control, they began to let go and fall over and the chain broke up.

Before long, only Magda, Bella, Sophie, Sid and William were left, whirling around at top speed.

Bella felt dizzy but Magda wouldn't stop. Suddenly, to her horror, Bella saw William shooting off the end of the chain and flying up, up, up into the air.

Bella screamed and at last Magda came to a halt.

Fortunately, William was OK. He'd landed on a man with a toothbrush moustache, a tweed jacket and a squashy tummy, who sat down with a bump in the playground.

"Who's that?" asked Bella.

"Mr Smart."

Bella gulped.

Even Magda looked nervous.

Mr Smart placed William on his feet and got up and dusted himself down.

Then he turned to Magda and Bella and barked, "You two. My classroom.

"NOW!"

FIRST
IMPRESSIONS

Mr Smart folded his arms and glared down at Bella and Magda.

"I used to be in the army, you know," he announced in a BIG BOOMING voice. "Now this is my parade ground and you are my soldiers."

Bella looked around in surprise. It didn't

look like a parade ground. It looked like a classroom. A very tidy and organised one.

"Order is what I like," he continued. "Order and discipline."

Bella could see that. It was immaculate.

The tables were arranged in rows of two and there wasn't a chair out of place.

On one wall, posters of times tables were pinned up with military precision.

On another, poems and stories in perfect

handwriting and carefully coloured-in pictures were displayed in straight lines. Bella couldn't help noticing that most of them had been done by Claudia Cleverley or Hetty Snoop.

"Eyes to the front!"

Bella quickly swivelled her eyes back to Mr Smart.

Mr Smart regarded Magda and Bella sternly.

"Magda! What have you got to say for yourself?"

"Sorry, sir. I was showing Bella how to play Spin Around."

Mr Smart turned his attention to Bella. Bella's legs turned to jelly.

"Whose class are you in?" he asked.

"Yours, sir."

Mr Smart looked confused. "Really? I don't remember you."

"I wasn't there this morning," admitted Bella bravely. "I was late."

"*Late?*" Mr Smart sucked in his breath and grew taller and straighter. "And *why* were you late?"

"Because I got stuck in Mrs Goodenough's classroom by mistake, sir."

"Mrs Goodenough." Mr Smart shuddered and deflated to his normal size.

"It's not Bella's fault, sir," piped up Magda. "It's her first day at school."

Magda is so brave, thought Bella as Mr Smart studied her with a frown. She could feel him taking in her yoghurt, toast, butter and marmalade-stained uniform.

Mr Smart pointed to the whiteboard and intoned loudly, "Rule number one: be punctual. Broken! Rule number two: wear your uniform with pride. Broken!"

He fixed Bella with his beady eyes. "Do you know what happens to pupils who break my rules?"

Bella shook her head mutely as her mind ran through various terrifying possibilities.

Sent to the Head?

Expelled?

Firing squad?

Mr Smart handed her two pieces of paper.

"Write out both of those rules twenty times by tomorrow and learn them by heart."

"Yes, sir."

Phew! Bella thought she'd got off lightly after all. Especially when Magda whispered to her, "I'll help you!"

CLAUDIA CLEVERLEY AND HETTY SNOOP

The bell rang for the end of playtime and the class started to line up outside the door. Mr Smart sprang into action.

"Right, young lady! We need to find you a seat."

"Can she sit with me?" asked Magda.

"Magda, you know the rules in this

classroom. Alphabetical order. What's your surname, Bella?"

"Button, sir."

"Typical." Mr Smart looked cross and Bella wondered how her name could possibly annoy him. Then he explained. "That's near the start of the alphabet so now I'll have to move everyone up one. That means you'll be next to ..." Mr Smart did a quick calculation in his head. "... Claudia Cleverley."

"But that's not fair!" said Magda. "That means I'll be sitting next to Hetty Snoop!"

"Enough, Magda," barked Mr Smart. "Let everyone in. Bella, you sit here."

Magda opened the classroom door and the children walked in in single file.

"That's my seat!" said a cold, clear voice.

Bella looked up to see a girl glaring down at her. She had straight fair hair cut into a neat bob, a pert little nose that stuck up at the end and a big bow in her hair that matched her ice-blue eyes.

"Take the next one, Claudia," said Mr Smart. "That's Bella's seat now. Everyone move up one."

Claudia flounced down next to Bella.

"Time for your spelling test," said Mr Smart, distributing pieces of paper. "Take

Mr Smart read out the spelling words one by one, Claudia had put her arm around her work as though she was afraid Bella would try to copy her.

There was no need. They weren't allowed to talk because it was a test or Bella would've told her she was:

Good at spelling.

Not a cheat.

Now was her chance to show her new teacher what she was made of. And, luckily for Bella, she knew them all.

"Swap your spellings with the person next to you," instructed Mr Smart when they'd finished. Then he wrote the correct spellings on the board and they marked each other's work.

"Now add up how many they've got right out of twenty and write an encouraging comment to them at the bottom of the page," continued Mr Smart.

Claudia had got one wrong but it was a hard one. Bella wrote *19/20* at the bottom of the page and *Well done!* in her very best writing. And then she added a smiley face.

To her surprise she noticed Claudia had

marked three words wrong on her test. She leaned over to inspect them.

"They're right," she said, puzzled.

"No they're not."

"Yes they are," Bella persisted. "*Receive* is *r-e-c-e-i-v-e*, *receipt* is *r-e-c-e-i-p-t* and *ceiling* is *c-e-i-l-i-n-g*. It's the rule: I before E, except after C."

"You wrote *i-e*."

"No I didn't. I wrote *e–i*."

"It's not my fault if your Es look like Is and your Is look like Es," said Claudia. "I'll correct them for you."

And before Bella could stop her, she'd written over them, pressing so hard you couldn't see the original letters underneath.

"All done," she said, and scrawled *17/20* and *Must try harder* on Bella's neat work. Then she jumped to her feet when Mr Smart asked for a volunteer to collect them in and put hers on top so he would notice her high mark.

"Well done, Claudia," said Mr Smart. "Top of the class again, I should think." Then he set them some homework on the board and, when they'd all copied it down, he dismissed them for lunch.

"Vomit!" said Magda, taking Bella by the arm and leading her off to the dining hall. "I bet Claudia cheated."

"How do you know?" asked Bella.

"She always does. So does Hetty Snoop, who sits next to me. But I fixed her."

"How?"

"I let her copy off me. And I got some wrong."

Bella's eyes widened. "Deliberately?"

"Well. Sort of."

Bella felt a whole lot better.

Outside the dining hall was a long queue. "Oh flip!" said Magda. "I'm starving!"

Bella was too. It seemed a long time since breakfast.

"Come on," said Magda. "Do what I say and you'll get served quicker."

She bypassed the queue and marched Bella straight up to the counter.

"This is Bella. She's new and she's gluten free," she announced.

"You've tried that one before, Magda," said Mrs Mole the dinner lady. "And dairy intolerance and nut allergy and vegetarian." She gave Bella a searching look. "You're not really gluten free, are you, sweetheart?"

Bella shook her head. She didn't even know what it meant. She hoped that she wasn't going to get into more trouble.

But Mrs Mole just laughed and said to Magda, "You're a caution, you are!" And she let them go first anyway, just this once.

TIME FOR TEA

Today Mum was picking up Bella and Sid from school because it was their first day.

"Oh good!" said Magda. "Can I get a lift too?"

Bella's heart missed a beat. Mum might still be cross with Magda after the yoghurt incident. Still, she wasn't going to say no, was she?

Lots of cars were waiting outside school.

"Look at that one!" Sid pointed to a long, low, open-topped sports car that was like something off a TV advert. The lady in the driving seat had streaked blonde hair and a sticky-up nose and she looked like Claudia Cleverley.

Next to it, their car looked old and battered.

"Mum? Can we take Magda home?" asked Bella.

"No," said Mum, and everyone's faces fell.

Then Mum laughed. "Look at your faces! We can't take her home because we're going to the café for a treat first. Jump in, Magda – you're coming too. I've cleared it with Babcia."

Bella, Magda and Sid cheered and tumbled into the back of the car.

"Which café are we going to?" asked Magda.

"Konrad's," said Mum.

Magda opened her mouth to speak but –

"Shhh!" said Mum with her finger to her lips, and Magda giggled.

"What's going on?" asked Bella.

"It's a secret," said Mum mysteriously, and off they went.

The café was in town. It was small and cosy and *very* busy. It had little metal tables, each with a jam jar full of wild flowers, sofas with colourful throws, and lots and lots of cushions. Sid sat on three while they waited to order. Everything

was pretty and nothing matched, not even the cups and saucers.

A waitress came out to serve them. She was skinny and smiley with a blonde ponytail.

"I want a whole chocolate cake!" demanded Magda immediately, which Bella thought was a bit rude.

So did the waitress. "Don't be greedy!" she said. "And sit up straight and take your elbows off the table."

Magda did as she was

told, and so did Bella and Sid.

This waitress is fierce, thought Bella, and wondered who she reminded her of.

"Mu-um!" moaned Magda.

So that was the secret! It was Magda's mum and dad's café.

"How do you do?" Magda's mum continued. "Welcome to our café. I am Krysia and my husband is the chef here. He is called Konrad."

"After the café?" asked Bella.

"Actually, it was the other way round," said Krysia as she took their order. "We only opened the café a few weeks ago. We work all day and half the night. We are lucky to have Babcia to keep an eye on Magda for us at home."

Her English was much better than Babcia's.

"It is good to meet you at last – I have heard so much about you. I hope Magda is not too much trouble?"

"Not at all," said Mum, who seemed to have totally forgotten about her sooty living room and the hole in her bedroom ceiling and her yoghurt-splattered car, and was more intent on deciding between a skinny latte or a decaf cappuccino.

In the end, Mum plumped for the latte, Sid chose a milkshake, and Bella and Magda opted for fruit smoothies. And, because it was the first day of school, Mum said they were each allowed a chocolate brownie for a treat.

When the order came, they stared at it in surprise. As well as the drinks and the chocolate brownies, there were delicate little sandwiches cut into nice shapes with yummy fillings like salmon and cream cheese, ham and tomato, and crab and cucumber.

"We didn't order these," said Mum worriedly as Krysia disappeared back into the kitchen.

But that wasn't all. She then brought out a *whole* cake stand with the top tier laden with cupcakes, the middle tier full of scones stuffed with jam and cream, and the bottom tier crammed with slices of lemon drizzle cake and raspberry and almond sponge.

They looked scrumptious.

Sid's eyes were wide with wonder but Bella's heart dropped. It seemed that Krysia's English wasn't so good after all. Now Mum would send them back and there would be trouble.

But Magda's mum said, "*Ta-dah!* Don't look so worried – they're on the house!"

"On the house?" asked Sid, puzzled. "What does that mean?"

"Complimentary," said Krysia, but Sid was none the wiser.

"Free!" explained Magda, and her mum nodded.

"First day at school is a special day. Enjoy your tea!"

So they did and it was delicious.

Afterwards, Krysia cleared the table and Bella and Magda did their homework while Sid, who was completely stuffed, had a snooze on Mum's lap.

Then Magda helped Bella write out Mr Smart's rules twenty times. Bella didn't even get into trouble with Mum because Magda said it was part of their homework.

Then they went home.

I'm so lucky to have Magda as my friend, thought Bella that night, as she checked that her bag was ready for school the next day. To her surprise she realised she was looking forward to it. And her homework was done so that was good.

But then she noticed that her homework book had Magda's name on it. She must have picked up the wrong book by mistake!

Never mind, Bella told herself sensibly. She could swap it in the morning.

Tomorrow, she and Sid and Magda were allowed to walk to school together!

She hoped Magda wouldn't be late.

PANCAKES FOR BREAKFAST

The next morning Bella and Sid didn't have to wait for Magda. Magda had to wait for them!

It was a bit hectic in the Button household.

Mum had left early, before anyone was up, and taken her car to go and visit

Granny, who lived a long way away. Dad was in charge.

The trouble was, he'd gone back to sleep after Mum left so everyone was running late. A lot late, actually. When Bella and Sid came downstairs dressed for school (Bella in a clean change of uniform after yesterday's messy start), he was in the kitchen in his business suit, shaving and talking on his phone at the same time.

"Can we have pancakes for breakfast?" asked Sid.

"Um … yes," said Dad. "Hold on, I'm speaking to work. I'll do them in a minute."

Sid couldn't believe his luck. They sat down to wait.

There was a knock at the door. It was Magda.

"Dad's going to make us pancakes!" shouted Sid.

"Yum," said Magda. "I love pancakes."

"Would you like some too?" asked Sid.

"Yes please," said Magda. "Can we have raspberries in them? From your garden?"

"Ye-e-e-ssssss!" shouted Sid, and he and Magda dashed out of the back door to pick them.

Dad carried on talking to work, pulling funny faces as he shaved. Bella was glad she didn't have to do that every morning. It took a lot of time.

Too much time.

Bella didn't want to be late for Mr Smart on her second day. Especially as she'd been late on her first. At least she was spick and span today.

The door burst open and Sid and Magda fell in, clutching handfuls of raspberries. Sid's face and new school shirt were covered in raspberry juice.

"We've got the raspberries. Where are the pancakes?" asked Magda, looking around.

"Shh …" said Dad, who had finished shaving at last but was still on his phone. "I'll do them in a minute. This is important."

He turned his back on them and carried on talking. Bella looked at the clock. That's what he'd said ten minutes ago.

"I can make pancakes," said Magda. "Where do you keep your flour?"

Bella's heart lifted. Of course she could – her dad was a chef. Bella wished her dad was a chef instead of an accountant.

She got out the big mixing bowl while

Sid rushed to the cupboard to fetch the flour.

"What else do you need?"

"Um, milk and eggs to make the batter, that's all. And oil to cook them in."

"I'll get them!" said Bella. *Thank goodness for Magda*, she thought, as she opened the fridge.

"Here you are, Magda," said Sid, placing a big, heavy, open bag of flour on the table.

On the edge of the table, to be precise.

He didn't push it in far enough. Bella turned around just in time to see it toppling over.

She and Magda lunged for it but it was too late. Instead Magda knocked the milk and eggs flying out of Bella's hands.

The flour exploded. Eggs and milk went everywhere.

Whumph! Splat!

On the walls.

On the floor.

On Bella's nice clean school uniform.

Bella screeched in horror.

Dad turned around and groaned. "Got to go!" he said into the phone.

The four of them stood in the kitchen surveying the damage. Not only were the floor and walls splattered with flour, eggs and milk, but so were they. Bella had come off the worst. Dad looked funny. His hair was white with flour and his smart business suit looked like it was covered in dandruff.

Only Bella didn't feel like laughing.

"We could mix it up on the floor?" suggested Sid, who still wanted his pancakes.

"It's too late for that," said Dad glumly. "Go and get changed while I clean this lot up and then I'll run you to school in my car."

LATE AGAIN

Not a good start to the day, thought Bella gloomily as she pulled yesterday's uniform out of the wash basket. Now it wasn't just stained – it was crumpled as well. But it was better than today's, which was spattered with batter ingredients and sopping wet.

It took a long time getting the flour and

milk and eggs out of her hair. It stuck like paste to her cornrows. In the end she tried to wash them under the tap.

By the time Bella got downstairs, with dripping hair and crumpled uniform, the others had cleaned themselves up (more or less), had breakfast (cereal, not pancakes) and were ready to go.

"Hurry up, Bella!" said Magda. "We're going to be late!"

Bella hesitated. Magda had had two breakfasts and she hadn't even had one. But she didn't want to be late for school so she grabbed an apple and said, "Let's go!"

At least Dad was giving them a lift. And as Bella crunched on her apple her mood lifted. They should get there just in time.

Outside school, cars were parked on both sides of the road, leaving only a single line of traffic able to get through. Mr Smart was in the playground.

"Quick!" said Magda. "He's about to ring the bell!"

Sure enough, he did. And all the children in the playground rushed to line up.

"I'll drop you here," said Dad. "Nip out quickly or we'll be blocking the road."

"Our bags are in the boot," Bella reminded him.

A car behind them honked furiously.

"Grr!" said Dad. He wound down his window and stuck his head out.

Magda wound down her window and stuck her head out too. "It's Claudia Cleverley's car!" she said in disgust.

"Hold on!" Dad shouted back to Mrs Cleverley. "I'll park over there in that space."

He put his indicator on and drove past the space to reverse into it. But Mrs Cleverley followed him and nipped in first.

Claudia jumped out of the passenger seat and ran in to join the line.

Dad swore loudly. Magda looked impressed.

Behind him another car tooted its horn.

"Sorry, kids, I'm going to have to go on," Dad said, and he kept on driving till he found a place to park.

It was a long way up the road.

By the time Bella, Magda and Sid had got their bags out of the car and run back to school, the playground was empty.

"We are going to be in SO MUCH TROUBLE!" said Bella desperately.

WHO FORGOT
THEIR HOMEWORK?

Sure enough, when she and Magda got into class, Mr Smart was VERY CROSS INDEED!

"Rule number one: be on time," he said, staring at his watch.

"Rule number two: wear your uniform with pride," he intoned, eyeing Bella's wet hair and stained, crumpled clothes with disapproval.

"Rule number three: be prepared," he added. "Have you done your homework?"

"Yes, sir," said Bella and Magda.

"You're lucky," he said. "Because if you break three school rules in one day you will be in VERY SERIOUS TROUBLE. Now sit down." He peered around the classroom. "Who would like to collect the homework in for me?"

Claudia Cleverley and Hetty Snoop shot their hands up before he'd even finished asking the question.

Bella fished her homework book out of her bag and remembered too late it was Magda's. Oh no! She'd forgotten to swap it in all the commotion of the morning.

Then she took a deep breath and tried to keep calm. It shouldn't matter. After all, they were all going in the same pile so Mr Smart would be none the wiser.

"All present?" asked Mr Smart when Claudia and Hetty brought the books out to him.

"Yes, sir," said Claudia, sounding disappointed.

Bella decided that she really didn't like Claudia Cleverley very much.

"No, sir," said Hetty. "Not quite."

A gasp went around the class.

Mr Smart folded his arms.

"Magda didn't hand her book in, sir," said Hetty smugly, smiling her superior smile.

Bella decided she didn't like Hetty Snoop either, with her silly floppy bow that was a carbon copy of Claudia Cleverley's.

They were both the kind of people who loved it when others got told off.

"Does that mean she's in VERY SERIOUS TROUBLE?" Claudia asked Mr Smart, her pert little nose twitching in excitement.

"Are you going to send her to the Head?" asked Hetty, her long thin nose quivering in anticipation.

"That's enough, thank you, Claudia and Hetty!" said Mr Smart, looking very stern. "Did you forget to do your homework, Magda?"

"No!" declared Magda hotly. "I've done it!"

"She did, sir! I saw her!" added Bella bravely. What was Hetty up to? She knew the book was there. She'd handed it in herself.

Mr Smart tutted. "In that case, the evidence should be here." He began to check through the big pile of books one by one, while the whole class waited with bated breath.

"Here it is!" he said, and opened it up. "Magda's right. She's done her homework."

Both Hetty and Magda looked surprised.

"But, but ..." protested Hetty.

Magda said nothing.

"Get your facts right, Hetty, and stop wasting my time," Mr Smart said crossly. "I think you owe Magda a big apology!"

"Sorry, Magda," spluttered Hetty, and everyone in the class looked pleased. Even mean old Claudia Cleverley who was supposed to be her friend!

Everyone, that is, except for Bella.

Because something *really* terrible had just occurred to her!

MAGIC AND SPELLS

"Magda, I need to talk to you!" said Bella at playtime.

But the next second, Claudia Cleverley and Hetty Snoop had marched up to them.

"How did you do it?" demanded Hetty.

"Do what?" asked Magda.

"Make your book appear like that? You couldn't find it in your bag. Then all of a sudden there it was, in the pile."

"Magic," said Magda. "I can do magic tricks. Actually, I'm a witch. I'm going to cast a spell on you two and turn you into fat, slimy slugs. Oh no, I forgot – you already are."

"Ha, ha!" said Hetty, but she looked a bit nervous.

"We're not scared of you and your silly little friend," said Claudia scornfully.

"Are you sure? I can do it, you know."

Magda bent down, picked up a snail and began to rub its shell, chanting all the while in a croaky voice:

"*Abracadabra, my little snail,*
Make a spell that will not fail.
Sticks and stones and stinky mud,
Toads' legs and lizards' blood.
A pinch of snot and
a bucketful of sick,
Mix it up to do the trick.
Add dead fish eyes and
crushed-up bugs,
Turn Hetty and Claudia
into slimy slugs."

Wow! thought Bella. *Magda is really good at making up spells.*

Hetty, who was not quite as brave as Claudia, backed away.

"Very funny," said Claudia, but even she sounded a bit uncertain. "Come on, Hetty!" And the two of them marched off, arm in arm.

Magda giggled and turned to Bella.

"I'm not really a witch. I haven't got a clue how my book appeared out of nowhere. It wasn't in my bag when I looked. I thought I must have left it at home."

"You did," sighed Bella. "After we did our homework in the café last night you took my book home by mistake. *I* handed in *your* book."

"Phew! Thanks, Bella," said Magda with a big smile.

Then her face changed.

"But that means ..."

"You've left *my* book at home! And now I'm in VERY SERIOUS TROUBLE! Mr Smart will think that I haven't done my homework," said Bella, looking miserable. "Oh Magda, what should I do?"

"Get Claudia's book, cross her name out and write yours on it instead," suggested Magda.

"I think he'd notice," said Bella.

"Hetty's?"

"Ditto."

Magda sighed. "You're right. Mr Smart is a stickler for homework. He takes it home every night to mark." Her face lit up. "That's it! What we must do is make sure he doesn't take it home tonight. Then tomorrow we can come to school early and slip your book into the pile before he gets here."

"That sounds like a good plan," said Bella. "But how do we stop him from taking the books home tonight?"

"Don't worry," said Magda comfortingly. "I'll think of something."

MAKING A PLAN

Throughout the day, Magda thought of lots of ideas to prevent Mr Smart taking their books home to mark. She told Bella all of them. They included:

- setting off the fire alarm
- turning on the taps and flooding the school

- starting a rumour that an earthquake was about to happen and the school would fall down
- asking the prime minister to pass a law to say that homework is banned
- telling Mr Smart that the government had declared books illegal so they all had to be burned immediately
- saying that the Queen had announced that today was a public holiday and no one was allowed to do any work, especially marking
- digging a pit on the school field and hiding all the homework books in it

🖋 locking Mr Smart in the
book cupboard overnight

🖋 letting the tyres down on his
car so he had to go home on
the bus and therefore he wouldn't be
able to carry all their books

🖋 telling him that a spaceship had
landed in the playground and an alien
had been seen running into school,
snatching Bella's homework book
and flying off again

🖋 standing up
in assembly and
shouting that a
herd of angry bison was heading this
way and they had to drop everything
and go home NOW!

There were lots more besides, most of them to do with fire and water and volcanoes and landslides and explosions and animals escaping from zoos and mad dogs and runaway trains. Each one was more extreme than the last and they were all 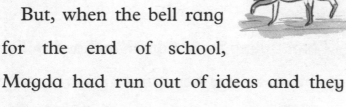 designed to separate Mr Smart from his marking.

But, when the bell rang for the end of school, Magda had run out of ideas and they still didn't know what to do. And to make matters worse, Claudia and Hetty had informed them that they'd counted the books on the teacher's desk and there was definitely one missing and they were going to tell Mr Smart.

Claudia jumped to her feet. "Shall I carry the homework books out to your car for you, sir?"

Bella felt sick with worry.

"No thank you, Claudia," said Mr Smart, reaching for his coat. "I'm not taking them home tonight."

The whole class stared at him open-mouthed.

"Not taking them home?" echoed Bella, unable to believe her ears.

"But, sir, there's one missing!" squeaked Hetty. "I've counted them!"

"And that means someone's not

prepared!" said Claudia triumphantly. "So, if they've already broken the first two rules, they should be sent to the Head."

Mr Smart groaned. "Hetty and Claudia, I haven't got time for this. I've got to dash off to a conference and I won't be back till the day after tomorrow. I'll sort it out then."

"Ohhh!" said Claudia sulkily.

"Does that mean we won't have a teacher tomorrow?" asked Magda, her eyes lighting up.

"You'll have a supply teacher," announced Mr Smart. "Now, everyone, I'm off." And with that, he was gone.

WALKING TO
SCHOOL

The next day, Bella and Sid walked to school by themselves. They were excited because they'd never been allowed to do it before. Where they used to live there were busy roads but here they could walk across the fields.

Magda was waiting for them at the gate. With her were Tom, who was in their class, and Kizzy, his sister, who was in the class below. They lived in the farmhouse down the lane and they looked alike. Tom had brown hair with a heavy fringe and Kizzy had the same plus bunches that stuck out at the side of her head.

Magda gave Bella her homework book. Phew! Bella tucked it safely into her bag in relief.

"I can't wait to see Claudia and Hetty's faces when they find out an extra book has appeared," chuckled Magda.

The five children made their way along the lane to a stile. From here a path led across the first field, which had black and white cows in it. Bella and Sid looked at the cows doubtfully. Close up they were really big.

"You're right to be careful of cows," said Kizzy, who seemed quite grown up for her age. "But it's OK – these are ours and we know them all."

"Follow me," said Tom. "I'll introduce you."

He picked up a piece of wood to use as a walking stick and led the way. They marched along the path in single file, singing a song that Tom taught them.

It went like this:

"Hey ho, hey ho,
It's off to school we go.
Past Brenda, Mo and Gert and Flo,
Hey ho, hey ho, hey ho …

Hey ho, hey ho,
It's off to school we go.
Past Ivy, Daisy, Em and Maisy,
Hey ho, hey ho, hey ho …"

And so it went on, over and over again,
until they'd named all
the cows. Then Magda
made up a rude verse
that went like this:

"Hey ho, hey ho,
It's off to school we go.
Past Claudia Cleverley and Hetty Snoop,
And lots and lots and lots of POOP!
Hey ho, hey ho, hey ho ..."

The cows joined in too, mooing and swishing their tails.

Soon they left the cows behind and marched through fields with houses backing on to them. More and more children spilled out of the houses to walk with them.

"This is like a walking bus!" said Sid, his eyes shining. It was fun. Much more fun than being driven along the road in a boring old car.

THE FAMOUS
ARTIST

When they got to school, Bella immediately tucked her book into the pile Mr Smart had left on his desk. Thank goodness that was over.

"Looking forward to being sent to the Head tomorrow when Mr Smart comes back?" asked Claudia sweetly as she and

Hetty walked into the classroom.

"Who, me?" asked Magda innocently. "What for?"

"Not handing your book in, of course."

"Magda's book was there, remember?" Bella pointed out bravely.

"D'you know what? I think you might have counted them wrong," said Magda. "Try again."

Claudia and Hetty's faces were a picture when they'd finished counting.

Hetty turned to Bella and eyed her suspiciously. "Somebody's book was missing, for sure. Someone must have added one. Was it you?"

Bella stared back at her mutely, praying that no one in the class would tell on her.

But nobody did, even though some people had seen Bella place it there.

"Good morning!" came a loud, jolly voice from the doorway, and everyone jumped. "I'm your teacher for the day. My name is Miss Pringle. Sit down, everyone!"

Everyone did as they were told, folded their arms like they did for Mr Smart and stared at her curiously. The teacher standing in front of them had lots of hair and bangles and beads and was very smiley.

"What a quiet and obedient class you are! Would someone like to tell me what you normally do?"

Claudia's hand shot up.

"Normally we learn something and then have a test on it. Normally I come top."

"Or I do!" interrupted Hetty.

The teacher looked surprised. "Well … today is going to be different."

Everyone perked up. Except for Claudia and Hetty.

"I'm an artist, you know," she continued. "And today we're going to let our hair down and HAVE FUN!"

Everyone cheered. Except for Claudia and Hetty.

"What sort of artist are you?" asked Hetty.

"A FAMOUS ONE!" laughed the teacher.

Claudia and Hetty sat up and looked interested.

Then the Famous Artist talked (a lot!) about FREE EXPRESSION and how she would like them to LET LOOSE THEIR IMAGINATION and EXPLORE THEIR CREATIVITY.

"Can we do anything we want?" asked Magda.

"Anything," said the Famous Artist.

Bella could see the ideas bubbling out of Magda's head.

"Can we work in pairs?" asked Claudia Cleverley.

"Of course."

"How long have we got?"

"All day." The Famous Artist looked at her watch. "Goodness me, is that the time already? We'd better get started."

As everyone jumped to their feet, she clapped her hands.

"I nearly forgot. At the end of the day I will choose the best project and put it on display in my studio for everyone to see. And … the winners will be in the local newspaper!"

Everyone cheered.

"That's us!" muttered Claudia Cleverley to Hetty Snoop. "We'll be famous like her!"

"Um … that's assuming your project is the best," said Magda.

"Of course it will be," said Claudia. "It always is. Please, Miss, shall we get the paints out for you?"

"Creep!" said Magda, but the Famous Artist didn't hear.

"That's very kind of you. Claudia and Hetty, isn't it?"

"Yes, Miss," said Claudia smugly.

She and Hetty got the paints out and took the best ones for themselves.

A SPOT OF
BOTHER

Magda and Bella got down to work straight away. Magda was bursting with ideas.

"Let's do a model of a mermaid. We'll make her tail out of fish scales and her hair from seaweed and her bikini top from seashells. Come on! I'll ask if we can go to the beach to collect them."

But the Famous Artist said they weren't allowed.

"We could make a dinosaur. One that moves, with flashing eyes."

But the Famous Artist said that might prove too difficult.

"We could make a car out of papier mâché. We did papier mâché in Mrs Goodenough's class. It's soggy paper that dries hard. Then we could take it to the garage and they could put an engine in and we could drive it!"

But the Famous Artist said perhaps that was a little too ambitious.

"I thought you said we could do anything we wanted?" said Magda, puzzled.

"Look, maybe you'd better stick to painting," suggested the Famous Artist, sounding just a teeny bit frazzled. "Get a move on. It needs to be finished today."

"We're doing a painting of you, Miss," said Hetty in her most oily voice, and Magda pulled a face.

"Come on, let's get some paints," said Bella. But when they looked on the table

there were only two pots left. One with a black top and one with a white top.

Everyone else had already started. Most people had paint pots with three or four different coloured tops.

Claudia and Hetty had paint pots with ten different coloured tops.

"Please can we have some of your paints?" asked Bella nicely.

"No!" snapped Claudia, putting her arms around the pots. "We need them all."

"We're going to win the competition," leered Hetty. "We're going to be in the paper."

"No, you're not – we are," said Magda grimly, and she and Bella moved off to the corner of the classroom with their two pots of paint.

"What can we paint that's black and white?" asked Bella.

"Um ... a newspaper?"

Bella shook her head.

"A zebra crossing?"

Bella shook her head again.

"A penguin?"

Bella shrugged. She supposed it was better than nothing.

"I know!" Magda's eyes shone. "Let's paint the cows. The ones we saw this morning!"

"Yes!" said Bella, and first she, then Magda, had a go at drawing a cow on a big piece of paper. It was harder than they'd thought. But Tom came to their rescue and sketched some out for them so they could start painting.

First they filled in the white patches very carefully indeed.

"That's looking nice!" said the Famous Artist.

Bella glowed with pride.

When the artist moved on, Claudia and Hetty came over to see.

"Huh! Fancy painting silly old cows!" said Claudia.

"You're a silly old cow!" said Magda, and even though it was a very naughty thing to say, everyone who heard her laughed.

Claudia went red with anger. And then she did something dreadful.

She picked up her paintbrush and deliberately flicked it at Bella and Magda's picture.

And Hetty, who was just as bad, copied her.

Bright blue and bright yellow paint splattered all over their beautiful picture.

Everyone who saw it gasped. Magda picked up the pot of black paint but, before she could empty it over their heads, the Famous Artist rushed over.

"What's going on?" she demanded, her hands on her hips.

"It was an accident," said Claudia, wide-eyed and innocent. "Sorry, Magda."

"We tripped," said Hetty, looking like butter wouldn't melt in her mouth. "Sorry, Bella."

The whole class knew that they were lying – except for the Famous Artist.

"Oh dear," she said sadly. "These things happen."

Magda glared at Claudia and Hetty. "This is sabotage," she said out of the corner of her mouth. "You're not going to get away with it."

But Magda was no sneak. When she turned to the Famous Artist, she didn't tell her what had really happened.

Instead, to Bella's surprise, she asked in a meek little voice, "Please, Miss, can we stay in at lunchtime to do it again?"

PUTTING
THINGS RIGHT

Bella and Magda were allowed to nip down to the dining hall before everyone else for an early lunch.

"You two first again? What's the excuse today?" asked the dinner lady. "Are you vegan? Vegetarian? Pescatarian?"

To Bella it was like she was speaking a foreign language. "What's a *pes-cat-arian*?"

"Someone who eats fish but not meat," explained Magda, and Bella remembered that her mum and dad ran a café. "No, we're allowed in first because we've got to stay in at lunchtime."

"Oh dear. You been up to no good?" asked Mrs Mole, cutting nice fat slices of pizza for them.

"Not yet," said Magda.

When Bella and Magda went back to the classroom, it was empty. Everyone else was at lunch. The Famous Artist had put a brand new, extra large piece of paper ready for them on the wall.

"We've got more colours to work with now," said Magda, helping herself to Claudia and Hetty's paint pots. "We can have a blue sky and green fields."

Bella couldn't get over how well Magda had taken the sabotage. She'd had to ask Magda what *sabotage* meant. Magda had explained that it was A DELIBERATE ACT OF DESTRUCTION, which made it sound very serious.

"Claudia and Hetty spoiled our picture because they thought it would win the competition. Don't worry. We'll get our own back on them.'

Bella thought it was very noble (and surprising!) of Magda to see that the best way to do that was by painting their picture all over again. But she couldn't help worrying it wouldn't be finished on time.

The door opened and Bella froze. Was

it Claudia and Hetty, intent on more sabotage?

It was Tom.

"D'you want some help with the cows?"

"Yes please!"

Quickly Tom sketched out two in the foreground and two in the background. There was no time for more.

"Can *I* paint them?" asked Magda. "Tom, you do the background, and Bella, you do the sky."

So the three of them started painting. Tom was very quick. Before long he'd finished his bit and went off to play football. The girls continued, Bella standing on a chair to do the sky while, beneath her, Magda concentrated hard on the cows.

"Getting there," said Magda, with satisfaction. "Oops! Now we've used Claudia and Hetty's paints we mustn't forget to top them up again."

To Bella's surprise Magda took the tops

off their paint pots, filled them up again and screwed the tops back on. Then she put them back where she'd found them.

Magda was so thoughtful. Bella felt Claudia and Hetty didn't deserve such kindness.

TRUE COLOURS

Everyone streamed back into the classroom.

"That's not fair!" Claudia Cleverley scowled when she saw that they'd nearly finished their painting. "They've had more time than us."

"They had to start all over again because of your clumsiness," said the Famous Artist, who was beginning to get the measure of Claudia and Hetty. "Now hurry up and finish off."

"I've just got to paint your lovely blonde hair, Miss," simpered Claudia, trying to get back on the right side of her. She dipped her brush into the pot with the yellow top.

"And I've got to paint your lovely blue eyes," gushed Hetty, dipping her brush into the pot with the blue top.

This is what happened next.

Claudia and Hetty started painting.

Claudia and Hetty screeched so loud the whole class came running to see what had happened.

Bella stared in surprise at the picture of the Famous Artist.

She had a streak of bright purple in her hair and one red eye!

"They've made you look like a zombie, Miss," observed Magda.

"Or a vampire!"

"Or a witch!"

"No, a ghost!"

"No, a ghoul!"

"What's the difference between a ghost and a ghoul?"

"She looks like a goblin to me!"

Everyone was shouting out and laughing.

"That's enough!" cried the Famous Artist, who was staring,

horrified, at her portrait. "That's not very flattering. I don't think I'd like that picture to be on display for all the world to see."

"How did it happen?" asked Claudia, looking perplexed. Then her face changed and she looked furious. "Oh I know. Someone's filled the pots up with the wrong paint on purpose! I bet it was Magda.'

"Or Bella!" Hetty glared at her.

The Famous Artist turned to them.

"Bella? Did you put the wrong paint in Claudia and Hetty's pots?"

"No, Miss," said Bella, round-eyed with shock.

"Magda? Did you? Now, tell me the truth."

"No, Miss," said Magda. "I swear on my honour and my mum and dad's café, I never filled the pots up with the wrong paint."

She sounded completely sincere. If Bella didn't know better, she would have believed her.

The Famous Artist studied them both with her arms folded.

Magda studied her back.

"They're lying. Send them to the Head, Miss," said Claudia spitefully.

Beside her, Bella, even though she hadn't done anything, was quaking in her shoes. It was Magda who'd filled the paint pots up, but now *she* was going to get into trouble too.

Then, to her surprise, the Famous Artist said, "We don't have time for wild accusations. Claudia and Hetty, hurry up and paint over it. The rest of you, get on with your work."

Bella breathed a huge sigh of relief. They weren't going to get in trouble after all.

Then the door opened and a head popped around it.

Not just any old head. It was the Head's head.

The class fell silent.

"Excuse me, Miss Pringle," said the Head. "Could I speak to Bella Button?"

IN THE HEAD'S OFFICE

Bella followed the head teacher to her office with her heart thudding.

She was in BIG TROUBLE!

Claudia and Hetty must have gone to her office at lunchtime and reported her for not doing her homework, which was three broken rules. What was worse, when the truth came out about Magda swapping the paints and ruining their painting she'd probably get blamed for that as well!

The Head held the door open and told Bella to take a seat.

Bella did as she was told, her knees knocking. She was about to be expelled!

"Would you like a drink, Bella?" the Head asked. "And perhaps a biscuit?"

She held out a packet of chocolate Hobnobs and Bella took one, mute with surprise.

"I like to have a little welcome chat with all my new pupils. How are you settling in, my dear? Making friends? I hope everyone's being kind to you?"

Bella choked on her biscuit.

The Head poured her a glass of water and told her that she had moved house and started a new school when she was Bella's age and how hard she had found it.

Then she said, "Tell me all about yourself."

So Bella took a deep breath and told her all about Mum and Dad and Sid, and her new very best friend Magda, and her new house, which was an old house, really, and the ghost in the attic, and Konrad's Café, and walking to school with Tom and Kizzy.

On and on and on she went, until the Head suddenly looked at her watch and said, "Goodness me! Is that the time?"

Then she said, "You can come and talk to me any time you want to, Bella. My door is always open."

Then she ushered her out and closed the door firmly behind her.

Bella walked back to her classroom feeling much better. To her surprise, only Magda was there, putting the finishing touches to their painting.

"Where is everyone?"

"They've all finished. Miss sent them out to play. I think she's gone for a quick lie-down. She said I could stay in and finish our painting."

"Let's see!"

But Magda stood in front of it with her arms wide and said, "No! It's a surprise! How did you get on with the Head?"

"She gave me Hobnobs."

"She gave me them too when I came to the school."

I'm going to like it here, thought Bella.

AND THE
WINNER IS...!

The Famous Artist clapped her hands.

"OK, everyone. Time's up. Now I need
to select the winning project. By the way,
who would like to stay behind and help
me clear up afterwards?"

Hetty and Claudia's hands shot up.

Magda rolled her eyes. "They're just

sucking up so she picks theirs. They've got no chance."

But Bella thought their picture was looking much better now. The Famous Artist had helped them paint over it. She didn't look like a zombie or a witch or a ghoul any more. She looked like herself again. Though perhaps not at her best.

Her face was smudgy grey where the purple had run and her eye was still a bit red. She looked like a tired, baggy-eyed version of herself, the way Bella's mum looked after a night out.

To be honest, the Famous Artist was looking a bit grey, tired and baggy-eyed in real life too. Working with children on FREE EXPRESSION, EXPLORING

THEIR CREATIVITY and LETTING LOOSE THEIR IMAGINATION had proved far more exhausting than she'd anticipated.

She examined all their paintings and said nice things about them, even if they weren't very good. But Bella could tell she'd had enough and just wanted to get home to a nice cup of tea.

The last one she looked at was theirs. Bella held her breath as the Famous Artist stood back and stared at their painting. Then she moved close, lifting her glasses and peering intently at the cows.

"Who did this?" she spluttered.

Bella's heart sank. What had Magda done now?

The Famous Artist's shoulders started to shake and she let out a honking noise like a donkey.

Bella stared at her in horror as tears poured down her cheeks. It was something so bad it had made her cry! They would be in real trouble now.

"Ohhhhh!" groaned the Famous Artist, holding her sides. "Oh, dear me! This is the funniest thing I've seen in years!"

The Famous Artist was laughing, not crying!

"I do enjoy humour in art," she said, with a hiccup. "Who can spot the subtle comic touch?"

Everyone leaped forward to examine the painting closely. Bella wondered what was so funny about it. It looked nice. Tom had painted the grass and flowers beautifully, her sky was blue with fluffy white clouds and Magda had done a good job on the cows.

UH-OH! Magda had done a *really* good job on the cows. Especially the two in the background.

One by one, people began to titter, then chuckle, then hoot and then howl. It was very contagious. Some people were doubled up; some people were even rolling around on the floor. A big roar of laughter filled the room as everyone got the joke.

Everyone, that is, except for Claudia Cleverley and Hetty Snoop.

The two cows in the background were

each wearing a jaunty blue bow tied round their right ear, exactly the same as Claudia and Hetty's.

And when you looked closely, one of them had a sticky-up nose, just like Claudia, and the other had a long, pointy nose, just like Hetty.

It was unmistakeably them.

And, best of all, beneath each one was a steaming pile of cow poo!

TELLING THE
TRUTH

"I told you we were going to win!" Magda
was triumphant on the way home. "Thanks
for helping us, Tom."

"No worries. It was worth it to see their
faces."

"They didn't like staying behind to
clear up," recalled Bella.

"Serves them right! They offered!"

"Only so the Famous Artist would choose their painting. And then she chose ours instead and they were really cross!"

"We're going to be famous," gloated Magda. "Our painting will be on display in her studio and we'll be in the newspaper."

"So will they, just like they wanted," pointed out Tom. "Only they'll be *in* the picture instead!"

Everyone laughed.

Bella thought how nice it was to be walking home from school together. Magda, Tom, Kizzy, Bella and Sid. She felt like one of the Famous Five, especially when Fetch, Tom and Kizzy's dog, ran up to greet them, wagging his tail. Though,

actually, that made them the Famous Six.

She was glad she'd moved to the countryside.

She was glad she was at her new school.

She was especially glad she had a best friend next door.

Magda was exciting and funny and honest and brave and not scared of anyone.

Only …

Bella sighed. Something was bothering her.

When Tom and Kizzy said goodbye and continued down the lane to their farm, and Sid rushed in to see Mum, Bella

waited at the gate. There was a question she had to ask.

"Magda? Tell me the truth. Did you really fill Claudia and Hetty's paint pots up with the wrong paint?"

Magda blinked at her in surprise. "No, of course not. I swore on my honour and my mum and dad's café. Didn't you hear me? I don't tell lies."

"I'm sorry," said Bella. "I didn't think you did. But the trouble is, I don't understand how the yellow paint came out purple and the blue paint came out red."

"Easy. I never switched the paints," said Magda, grinning from ear to ear. "I swapped the lids instead."

READ BELLA AND MAGDA'S
NEXT ADVENTURE IN

TROUBLE ON THE FARM

COMING AUGUST 2018

CHRIS HIGGINS began writing

young fiction when she rapidly acquired a

whole bunch of grandchildren, and is

the author of the *My Funny Family* series.

Chris has travelled the world and lives

in Cornwall with her husband.

Her books for Bloomsbury are *Trouble*

Next Door and *Trouble At School*.

EMILY MACKENZIE is an
award-winning illustrator and keen knitter.
She is the author and illustrator
of *Wanted! Ralfy Rabbit, Book Burglar* and
Stanley the Amazing Knitting Cat.
Emily lives in Edinburgh.